DiNO RiDERS

How to Tame a Triceratops

Don't miss:

How to Rope a Giganotosaurus
How to Hog-Tie a T-Rex
How to Catch a Dino Thief

DINO RIDERS

How to Tame a Triceratops

Will Dare

sourcebooks
jabberwocky

Published by Sourcebooks Jabberwocky, an imprint of Sourcebooks, Inc.
P.O. Box 4410, Naperville, Illinois 60567-4410
(630) 961-3900
Fax: (630) 961-2168
www.sourcebooks.com

Library of Congress Cataloging-in-Publication Data

Names: Dare, Will, author.
Title: How to tame a triceratops / Will Dare.
Description: Naperville, IL : Sourcebooks Jabberwocky, [2017] | Series: Dino
  riders ; 1 | Summary: With the help of his friends Sam and Abi and his
  trusty Dino Cowboy Diary, Josh dreams of roping a wild Triceratops and
  maybe become the next great Dino Rider.
Identifiers: LCCN 2016000712 | (alk. paper)
Subjects: | CYAC: Dinosaurs--Fiction. | Triceratops--Fiction.
Classification: LCC PZ7.1.D32 Ho 2016 | DDC [Fic]--dc23 LC record available
at https://lccn.loc.gov/2016000712

Printed and bound in the United States of America.
VP 10 9 8 7 6 5 4 3

With special thanks to Barry Hutchison.

CHAPTER 1

I t was 8:00 a.m., and Josh Sanders was sitting on a dinosaur.

This wasn't unusual. He sat on a dinosaur almost every morning. In fact, most people in the Lost Plains did. But Josh had been in his saddle for a while now, and his butt was beginning to ache.

"Plodder," Josh moaned as he wriggled in his seat. "You're about as comfy as a cactus!"

Plodder kicked his feet and snorted into the air. A gooey trail of dino snot splattered onto the ground.

"Ew!" Josh laughed. "And you're gross!" He gave the gallimimus a friendly pat on the side. "C'mon, buddy. We've got iguanodons to find. We can't sit around here all day!"

Josh made a clicking noise with his mouth and nudged the dinosaur with the heel of his boot. Slowly, he began to move forward. In the distance, Josh could see the huge fence that kept the predators out. Well, most of them. No fence this side of the Lost Plains could keep out a T. rex.

"Come on, Plod," he urged, rocking in the saddle. "Sometimes, I think it'd be quicker if *I* carried *you*!"

Plodder was a long-necked, reliable gallimimus, used for herding iguanodons—but he was getting old now. Josh would do anything for a faster dino. His hero, Terrordactyl Bill, rode around on a triceratops, protecting the Lost Plains from fearsome dinosaurs and criminals. He was the greatest dino rider ever. Legend had it he'd once knocked out a brontosaurus with a single punch. Josh smiled at the thought of T-Bill in action. Now *that* would be an exciting life.

Eventually, Josh spotted the group of iguanodons he was after. They were wandering near the edge of the Sanders' Ranch territory, right where the predators roamed. It was Josh's job to herd them back where they belonged. With their bulky bodies and lumbering walk,

iguanodons weren't the fastest dinosaurs, but they sure could beat you up if you didn't treat them right.

"OK, Plodder," he cried. "It's time for some action!"

Unclipping the rope from his belt, Josh gave it a twirl above his head.

Ker-ack!

Josh snapped the lasso like a whip in the air behind the iguanodons. At once, a deep roar went up from the herd, and the beasts broke into a run.

"Now we're talking. Let's go!"

As Josh yanked on the reins, Plodder hollered and set off in pursuit. Josh felt the ground shake as the heavy iguanodon herd grunted and snorted, thundering across the plains and back toward the ranch. As the sun rose above the Wandering Mountains in the distance, he let out a whoop of joy.

"Woo-hoo!" he yelled, raising the rope above his head once more. His hat flew backward, and he felt the wind whistling through his sandy hair. Sometimes, riding Plodder wasn't so bad after all!

He moved toward the iguanodons, gently steering them in the right direction and dodging in and out of their gigantic legs and stinky bodies. However, as most of the iguanodons made their way back toward their pen, Josh suddenly noticed one of the big brutes veering off from the herd.

"Uh-oh," he muttered. A knot of panic tightened in his chest. This one dinosaur was running away from the others, right in the direction of the Sanders' farmhouse.

"Get back here, you oversize lizard!" Josh called, but he knew words were no use. If the out-of-control dinosaur kept going, the house would be smashed to pieces.

This called for action.

Josh squared his shoulders and narrowed his eyes. *What would Terrordactyl Bill do?* he thought.

Suddenly, he had it.

"Yah!" Josh cried, digging his boot heels against Plodder's ribs. The dino shot forward, and they thundered up a slope in quick pursuit.

Dust clouds rose up from the iguanodon's heavy claws and clouded Josh's vision. He pulled on the reins to dodge from left to right.

Plodder grumbled as Josh flicked the reins but managed an extra burst of speed. They caught up with the iguanodon just as it crashed through a wooden fence, sending splinters flying through the air.

"Not on my watch," Josh growled, doing his best T-Bill impression. He grabbed his lasso and raised it above his head. He twisted his wrist, and the rope twirled through the air.

Josh let the lasso go. It flew through the air and looped expertly around the iguanodon's neck.

"Gotcha, big guy," cried Josh, pulling back

on the guano. "Now, are you going to come quietly or—*whoa*!"

Suddenly, Plod began to slow down. The iguanodon, on the other hand, was just getting started. It charged forward, almost dragging Josh out of the saddle. Josh was being pulled in two different directions.

"Argh!" he cried. "Plod! Don't give up on me now!"

It was no use. His dinosaur was struggling to keep up. Josh had to do something.

In one swift move, he leaped up out of the saddle and stood on Plodder's back. He balanced on the old dino like he'd seen them do at the rodeo, all the while grabbing the lasso tightly. As the two dinosaurs thundered along,

9

Josh bent low, then jumped forward for all he was worth.

"Get back here!" he yelled as he sailed through the air and landed on the charging iguanodon.

The dinosaur reared and cried out, but Josh held on tight.

With a desperate heave, he dragged himself farther up until he straddled the giant beast. As he got his balance, he looked forward and let out a yelp of shock. The house was approaching fast.

"Stop!" Josh yelled, yanking on the lasso. He pulled with everything he had.

The iguanodon let out a huge bellow from the depths of its belly.

Muuu-ahhhhh-rrrrr!

Just as the iguanodon was about to smash into Josh's front porch, Josh yanked as hard as he could to the left. At the last moment, the exhausted iguanodon veered to the side, giving up its one-dinosaur stampede, and came to an abrupt stop.

"Hee-yah!" Josh cried triumphantly. "I told you I'd—"

But before he could finish, the iguanodon had one last trick. It kicked up its hind legs and launched Josh off its back like a cannonball. His grip slipped on the rope, and he was hurtled through the air. With a soggy *schlopp*, he landed headfirst in a pile of dino dung.

Josh, dripping with muck, grumbled under his breath. But then, he couldn't help but laugh

out loud and gave the iguanodon a hearty slap on the flank. "Nice try, mister. But you're no match for the wildest rider in town."

Josh heard a creaking noise from the porch, and a tall, thin shadow peered over him.

"What in the name of—"

As Plodder came slowly scuffing his way toward the ranch, Josh looked up with a grin. "Dad, I think I need a faster dino!"

CHAPTER 2

Once Josh's dad had helped round up the last of the iguanodons, it was time for school. They didn't talk about getting a faster dinosaur, but it was still on Josh's mind.

On the ride toward the Trihorn settlement, he met up with his friends Sam and Abi. After the morning's excitement, Plod was even slower than usual, especially compared to the dinos Josh's friends were riding. Josh didn't

worry though. He was too busy telling them all about what had happened.

"And then," he said, "the iguanodon bucked upward and—"

"Threw you into a pile of dung?" Abi asked, sniffing the air.

"How did you know?" Josh asked. "I took a bath!"

"Because you've told us twenty times," Sam said with a grin.

Josh laughed. Then his eyebrows scrunched together, and he wafted his denim shirt. "I don't still smell, do I?"

"No more than usual," Abi said with a grin.

Josh gave her a playful shove. Only Sam and Abi could get away with teasing a wannabe dino rider like him—they'd been friends forever. If anyone else had tried it, they would be toast.

"And anyway, it's just school," Sam added. "You don't need to smell good for that!"

Josh sighed. When he wasn't helping out on the family ranch or dreaming of being a dino

rider, he had to go to school like everyone else. As they got nearer to the Trihorn settlement, he saw the school building looming, and his stomach sank. It wasn't the same for his friends; Sam knew *everything*, and Abi loved making wisecracks to the rest of the class, whereas Josh wanted action and adventure. Didn't they know there was a world of roaring dinosaurs, huge mountains, and scary valleys out there?

Suddenly, Josh saw something that made him feel even worse. Throwing up dust as it bounded toward them, a huge, club-tailed ankylosaurus came charging their way. Only one boy at school rode a dinosaur as mean as that: Amos Wilks.

"Uh-oh," Sam huffed. "What does he want?"

Josh bristled. Amos had been his all-time worst enemy ever since the bully had dumped diplodocus dung on Josh's head when they were five. He was only a few months older than Josh, but he was a lot bigger. Amos's pimply face sneered as he came closer.

"Hey, slowpoke," Amos called.

"What do you want?" Josh hissed.

"That's not very nice!" Amos said with a snarl. "I just came to ask if you wanted to ride on a *real* dinosaur like Clubber. With a *real* rider— like me!"

"This is a real dinosaur," Josh said, patting Plodder on the side. "And I am a real rider!"

20

"Really?" Amos went on. "You won't get far on him. He looks like he's about to fall asleep on his feet."

It was true. Plod did look a bit tired from rounding up the iguanodons. But that didn't mean Amos could make fun. Josh fumed.

"Oh yeah, well…" Josh tried to think of something to say but was completely tongue-tied.

"Ha-ha!" Amos laughed. "Good comeback, loser. I'll see you at school—if you ever get there."

Amos kicked at his dinosaur, Clubber, and charged off into the distance.

"Ugh, I hate that guy," Sam said. "Why does he have to be so mean?"

Josh felt the same way. His cheeks went red

with embarrassment. There had to be a way of showing Amos who was the best rider. If only he could think of a plan…

CHAPTER

3

Today, we're going to be learning about the weather," Miss Delaney announced, hovering in front of the blackboard.

Josh groaned. *The weather?* It rained. It was sunny. And sometimes it was in between. Surely, that was all they needed to know.

Josh took his dino-bone pen from his pencil case. Maybe she was going to talk to them about the cyclones and tornadoes that sometimes blew across the Lost Plains.

"Did you know," Miss Delaney asked, her green eyes glinting with excitement, "that there are different types of clouds?"

Josh frowned. Even the class's pet microraptor looked bored, idly flapping its wings in the corner.

Josh leaned under his desk and took a battered old iguanodon-skin notebook from his bag. *Dino Rider Handbook* was written on the front in red ink.

He'd gotten the notebook years ago, and every time he learned something new about dinosaurs, he'd write it in. He reckoned

it would come in very handy when he eventually became a lone rider like Terrordactyl Bill.

While Miss Delaney droned on, Josh added the finishing touches to a drawing of a T. rex.

After a few minutes of concentration, he realized the class had gone silent. Beside him, Sam gently cleared his throat.

Josh looked up. Miss Delaney stood over him, arms folded. "I make that the fourteenth time this week I've caught you not listening, Joshua Sanders," she said.

"I was listening!" Josh cried, leaning over his notebook to try and hide the picture.

Miss Delaney frowned. "Oh really? Is that a cloud you're drawing? What's its name?"

Josh swallowed. "Er…Bob?" he muttered.

The rest of the class started to giggle.

Miss Delaney shook her head and sighed. "Are you listening to me now, Josh?"

Josh nodded.

"Good, because I have an important announcement to make that even you might find interesting!"

She returned to the front of the class and unrolled a poster. "As you all know, next weekend will mark the one-hundredth anniversary of the Trihorn settlement."

A few murmurs went up from the classroom.

"That's right! One hundred years of the Trihorn settlement's existence here in the Lost Plains, nestled between the Wandering Mountains and the Roaring Jaws Valley. One

hundred years of surviving against the T. rex threats and everything else that nature has thrown at us. So the mayor is planning a Founders' Day celebration. And to mark the occasion, there's going to be a race…"

Josh sat bolt upright. This *was* interesting.

"…across some of the toughest and deadliest predator-filled terrain there is…"

Josh couldn't believe his ears. This was his chance to prove once and for all that he was a better dino rider than Amos Wilks. But then, Mrs. Delaney said something that made it even better.

"And the first prize trophy will be presented by none other than the wildest dino rider in the Lost Plains: Terrordactyl Bill himself!"

CHAPTER 4

Josh sat at the breakfast table on Saturday morning, munching on one of his mom's famous breakfast pies. She bustled around the kitchen, humming merrily as she searched for her toolbox.

As he chewed, Josh studied a newspaper article about

Terrordactyl Bill. He still couldn't believe that he was coming to the Trihorn settlement. He had to be on the podium when T-Bill presented the trophy. Better yet, he had to win!

"Did you know," Josh began, "Terrordactyl Bill actually got himself swallowed whole by a T. rex? On purpose!"

"Did he?" his mom asked, smiling. "That sounds pretty dangerous."

"T-Bill isn't scared of danger! He ran right at it and jumped down its throat," Josh said, spraying lumps of his breakfast all over the paper. "All because it ate his favorite hat!"

"He does have a nice hat," his mom said.

Josh nodded. He looked over at his own hat hanging on the back of the kitchen door. It was an exact replica of T-Bill's, complete with wide brim and black band.

"How did he get back out?" his mom asked.

Josh shrugged. "Doesn't say."

"I hope it was through his mouth." She shook her head and plonked her tools on top of the counter. "So, what are you up to today, Josh Sanders?"

Josh swallowed. "Um, I'm going to go into Trihorn." He didn't want to reveal his plans to enter the race in case she said no. It was all he'd thought about since Miss Delaney announced it, and he didn't want to mess things up now. "I'm meeting up with Sam and Abi."

"Oh? And what are you all going to do?"

"Nothing."

His mom turned from the worktop. "Nothing?"

"Um…yeah." Josh nodded. His eyes darted to the door.

"You're up to something," his mom said.

Josh shook his head and gave her his most convincing smile.

His mom narrowed her eyes. "OK, then. Just you stay out of trouble."

Standing up, Josh gave a nod. "I always do."

"Well, we both know that isn't true," she laughed.

Josh unhooked his hat and pulled it on. He raced outside and jumped onto Plod, then rode off into town.

The Sanders' Ranch was only a couple of miles from Trihorn, the very center of the Lost Plains. When Josh got nearer, he saw that the streets were heaving with dinosaurs of all shapes and sizes. Gallimimuses trotted alongside coaches pulled by stegosauruses. Microraptors swooped back and forth on their four wings, delivering messages that were tied to their feet. Down on the ground, tiny scavenger dinos scurried around, dodging in and out of their larger cousins' legs.

"Morning, Josh!" called Mr. Watson, the owner of their neighboring ranch. He, his wife, and all six of their children sat on the back of a young brontosaurus that thudded along the main street, nudging the other dinosaurs out of its path. The brontosaurus's long neck

had eight saddlebags draped over it, each one bursting at the seams with supplies from the general store.

Josh waved and steered Plod out of the baby bronto's path. When it passed, he hurried through the gap it left and over to the town hall right in the center of Trihorn. Sam and Abi were sitting on their dinos, waiting for him.

"Are you sure about this?" Sam asked, looking at Josh nervously. "I haven't seen any other kids entering. Isn't it dangerous?"

Josh shook his head. "I eat danger for breakfast."

"I thought you always had pie for breakfast?" Abi frowned.

"It was just a… Forget it," Josh said,

dismounting from Plod and tying him to the tethering post outside the hall. A rickety wooden stand had been set up right by the main door. The deputy mayor stood behind it, beaming broadly at everyone who met his eye.

"Step right up," Mr. Geary urged, mopping his shiny brow with a handkerchief. "Sign up here for the great Founders' Day race, and earn your place in history!"

"You can sign me up!" said Josh eagerly.

The deputy mayor's smile grew wider, and his moustache danced on his top lip like a caterpillar.

"Well now, good for you, son!" he said, thumbing his suspenders. "But first, it's my duty to warn you what you're getting yourself into. Y'see, this here race is gonna be mighty dangerous."

"He eats danger for breakfast," said Sam, leaning over.

"And pie," Abi added.

The deputy mayor slapped his thigh and laughed. "Well now, that may be, but you ain't never encountered danger quite like this before." He put an arm around Josh's shoulders and held a hand out in front of him, as if painting a picture in the air. "The route takes you through twisting canyons, leaps you over near-bottomless pits, and has you battling against fellow racers and fellow dinosaurs, not just for victory but for your very survival!"

Josh swallowed. He glanced at his friends,

then back at the deputy mayor. "That sounds…
amazing! I'm in!"

"That's my boy!" The deputy mayor laughed.
"Now, what sort of dino are you ridin'?"

Josh jabbed a thumb toward Plodder.
"That one."

The deputy mayor's moustache drooped sadly as he looked Plodder up and down. "That old thing? You can't be serious."

"He's fast," Josh said in protest. "You know… sometimes. He *can* be fast."

"I'm sorry, son. You'll need a tougher dino than that if you wanna ride in this race."

Josh's smile drooped. Suddenly, he saw his dreams turn to dino dung right before his eyes. How was he ever going to be a dino rider, traveling the Lost Plains in search of adventure and dinosaurs, when he couldn't even enter the local race? And as if he didn't feel bad enough, suddenly, the ground shook beneath him.

"Enemy approaching," Abi muttered.

Kicking up a cloud of dust, a mean-looking dinosaur with a spiky club-like tail thudded up the street and stopped right beside Josh. From high on the beast's armored back, Amos called over to the deputy mayor.

"Hey, Mr. Geary. Sign me up for the race," he barked. "And be quick about it."

"Ugh," Sam said. "Who does he think he is?"

But Josh knew exactly who he thought he was. Amos's dad was the town mayor, which meant Amos thought he could boss around anyone he wanted—and he usually could.

Mr. Geary hurriedly scribbled Amos's name onto one of the forms he was grasping in his hands. "Sure thing, Master Wilks. It's my pleasure."

Amos turned his gaze on Josh. "Oh, please tell me you're racing too."

"Yes, I am," Josh said defiantly.

"No, he isn't," said Mr. Geary. "His dino's too slow."

Amos barked out a nasty laugh. "Yeah, that sounds about right."

Josh puffed out his chest. He wasn't about to let go of his dreams that easily, especially not in front of a barrel-chested bully like Amos. "Well, that doesn't matter," he said. "Because I'm not racing on Plodder. I'm riding another dinosaur."

"You don't have another dinosaur," Amos scoffed.

"Well...I'll get one," Josh said. "And then I'll win the race. Just you wait and see."

Amos smiled, showing a mouth full of yellow teeth. "In that case, may the best rider win!" he said with a snarl. He gave the deputy mayor a nod and then kicked his heel into Clubber.

"What are you going to do?" Abi asked. "I know Clubber looks heavy, but he's a pretty quick racer when he wants to be."

"And where are you going to get a new dinosaur?" asked Sam.

Josh stared after Amos, watching Clubber's dust cloud fade into the distance. "I don't know yet," he admitted. "But I know one thing for sure…" He turned and took the pen from the deputy mayor, then wrote his name on the form. "I'm gonna win me that race!"

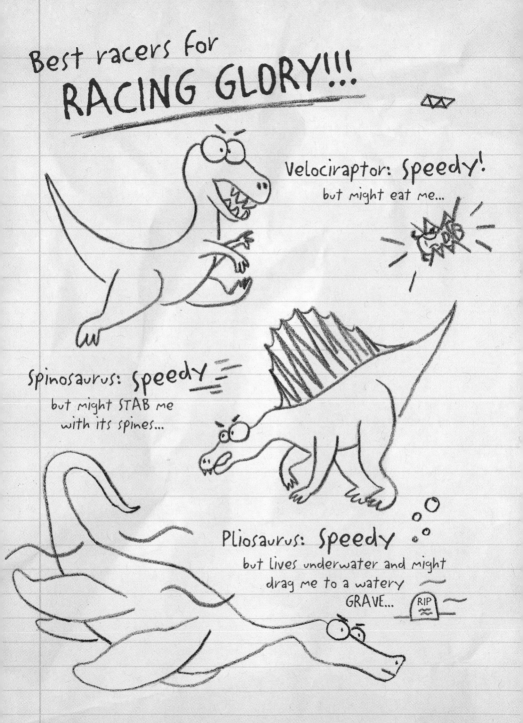

CHAPTER 5

Over the next few days, Josh searched high and low for another dinosaur to ride in the great Founders' Day race, but no one was willing to part with a dino this close to the big day. Good thing Josh had a plan.

He'd "accidentally" forgotten to tell his mom and dad about signing up for the race. So they'd given him a couple of iguanodons to trade at the market for a new roundup dino like Plodder. But Josh was going to buy a racer!

As Josh walked his family's huge iguanodons to the market along the Trihorn road, he clicked with his mouth or clapped his hands whenever they looked like they might wander off the path. The guanos were slow—and very gassy—and Josh dodged the stench whenever he could.

As he rounded the bend into the settlement, the dinos stumbled to a stop as a man in a top hat stepped into their path. His clothes were rumpled, and his hair stuck out beneath the brim of his tall hat. He smiled at Josh and then bowed deeply.

"Top of the morning to you, lad," said the

man in a strange accent. "Name's William O'Donnell. A pleasure to meet you."

"Um, hello," said Josh. He knew he shouldn't speak to strangers, and this man seemed stranger than most. "Don't mind us…"

"Of course, of course," said William, stepping aside. "Although…you wouldn't be on your way to the market by any chance? To offload these fine iguanodons?"

"Yeah." Josh nodded suspiciously. "Why?"

"Oh, nothing at all. Don't mind me one little bit," said William. He gestured for Josh to pass, but before Josh could take a step, the man added, "Although, we may be able to help each other."

Josh looked puzzled. His sandy brows knitted together.

"Turn your eyes that way," William said, gesturing over to Josh's right. There, tethered to a post, was a huge, stocky dinosaur. Its shoulder muscles bulged as it munched on the grass at its feet. Its three curved horns shone in the sunlight.

Josh gulped. "A triceratops!"

"That's right. And a finer triceratops you couldn't hope to meet," said William. "Only problem is I have no need of one myself. What I'm after is a couple of fine iguanodons. You wouldn't know of anyone interested in making such a trade, would you?"

"But a triceratops is worth at least five guanos." Josh blinked in surprise. He couldn't have hoped for such a good deal at the market.

He suddenly had visions of himself riding alongside T-Bill with a triceratops of his own. Although, he'd never heard of a triceratops making a good roundup dino before. He wondered what his dad would say.

"I know… And this one especially," the man continued. "Charge is the name. He's as swift as a bullet in a hurricane. Someone will get themselves a real bargain," said William, tipping his hat. "So if you hear of anyone looking to make a deal, you send them my way."

Josh watched the man stroll off in the direction of the triceratops. He looked down at the guanos, just as one of them loudly broke wind. All he'd find at the market would be another gallimimus, and everyone in the Lost Plains had one of those. But Charge was one of a kind. Surely his parents would see that?

And besides, triceratops were fast. Really fast.

"I'll make that trade!" Josh said hurriedly, chasing after William.

William stopped in his tracks. He spun on the spot and threw his arms out wide. "Ah, that's grand. You've got yourself a real bargain to be sure." He slipped a couple of ropes over the necks of the iguanodons and backed away quickly, almost dragging the lizards along with him.

"A pleasure doing business with you, lad," William said, hurrying along the path as fast as his legs could carry him. Just before he vanished around a bend, Josh could've sworn he heard the man shout, "Good luck!" but he didn't think anything of it.

Josh made his way over to the giant triceratops and took hold of his rope. The muscly brute of a dinosaur gave a snort that nearly blew off his replica T-Bill hat.

"Wow!" Josh gasped in awe when he'd gotten over Charge's stinky breath. "Just wait 'til Amos Wilks sees this beauty…"

He gave a tug on the rope to get Charge moving, but the triceratops just lowered its enormous head and chomped on a mouthful of grass. It chewed slowly, not paying Josh any attention at all.

"Come on," Josh urged, but Charge flopped down on the grass and yawned. Lying down, the dinosaur was still taller than Josh. Muscle rippled beneath its broad back and up to the shoulders where it met Charge's hard, armored fringe.

Digging his heels into the ground, Josh heaved on the rope. "Move!" he shouted. Charge blinked lazily then snorted through both nostrils, spraying Josh in a mist of dino snot.

"That does it, mister," he said. "You're coming with me!" Josh rolled up his sleeves and yanked, but nothing happened.

Suddenly though, a loud shriek echoed in the distance. A microraptor, on one of its postal errands, flew overhead. Charge snapped to attention, springing to his feet like an eager dog. Josh felt the world lurch sideways as the

triceratops broke into a run, chasing after the flying 'raptor.

"Waaaargh!" Josh wailed, bouncing along on the end of the rope. Charge kicked and thrashed and spun. The rope burned at Josh's hands as Charge dragged him halfway along the road and into a field full of corn.

"Stop!" Josh cried.

As the microraptor surged into the distance,

Charge abruptly came to a stop. Josh scooped sticky mud from his face as Charge stood watching him, his tongue hanging out as he panted excitedly.

Josh, gasping for breath, carefully approached the triceratops. "So now I really know why they call you Charge!" he said with a laugh.

CHAPTER 6

The next day at school, Josh paid even less attention than usual. He was supposed to have been studying the geography of the Scratchclaw Swamps, but instead, he'd spent most of the day secretly scribbling in his notebook. While the teacher droned on, Josh had written *How to tame a triceratops* at the top of one of the pages. Below that, he planned to list all the

How to tame a triceratops:

1.) Erm...
2.) Ask it nicely?

different ways he might be able to get Charge under control.

Unfortunately, he couldn't think of any, so it was a very short list.

When Josh had come home with a triceratops, he thought his parents would be as excited as he was, but instead, they'd hit the ranch roof. He was supposed to buy a roundup dino, not a racer, and he'd had to come clean about the whole plan. He could still hear his dad's words ringing in his ears: "Unless you get that three-horned brute of a dino under control and fit for ranching, you're not entering that race, Joshua Sanders!"

He imagined Amos Wilks winning the race and getting to meet T-Bill, and his heart sank.

"Your mom and dad still mad?" Sam asked as they filed out of the class and untied their dinos from the tethering post.

"You could say that," Josh replied, his face creased with worry. "I have to think of *something*. The whole race depends on it!"

"What about food?" Sam asked, determined to help his friend. "That's what my mom uses to get me to do what she wants!"

"Maybe!" Josh said, brightening a little. He pulled the remains of his lunch out of his school bag and waved it in the air in front of Charge. "Look what I've got, buddy," he said, holding a piece of his mom's home-made pie.

Slurp! Charge's tongue flicked out and

scooped up the whole thing. He swallowed it without even chewing, then let out a loud, rumbling burp that blew Josh off his feet.

Abi laughed. "How's the bribery working out for ya?"

"Hmm, not quite as planned," Josh said.

"How about giving him a good scratch?" Sam suggested.

Josh picked up a broom that was propped against the school wall and approached Charge from behind. Plodder used to love a good scratch behind the ears, so he was sure that Charge would appreciate it too.

"Got an itch, boy?" Josh asked. He crept closer, holding the brush out in front of him. When he was just a foot or two away, he used

the hard bristles to scratch the triceratops's broad back. "There. How's that feel?"

Wham! Charge's back leg shot out, hitting Josh in the belly. Josh doubled over, staggering back and gasping for breath. "Ow!" he said and wheezed.

"That actually went much better than I expected," said Sam, coming out from behind his own dino, Nickel.

"Yeah," Abi laughed. "At least you're still in one piece!"

"That's a shame…"

Suddenly, Josh heard a familiar snort of laughter from behind him.

"I got a real *kick* out of watching that," sniggered Amos Wilks.

A weasel-faced little figure crept out from behind Amos's back and giggled through his nose. It was Arthur, Amos's nasty sidekick. He was always hanging around, ready to do Amos's dirty work, even if Amos was mean to him as well.

"He-he. Yeah," Arthur said with a snigger. "A real kick!"

"Shut up, Arthur," Amos barked.

Arthur immediately shrank back in silence.

Josh turned to face the bully. "What do you want, Amos?" he demanded.

Amos puffed out his chest and glared down at the much smaller Josh. "Well now, that ain't exactly friendly, is it? I just came to see how you were getting on and to wish you luck—one racer to another."

"No, you didn't," said Abi, standing shoulder to shoulder with Josh. "You came here to spy on him."

"Because you're scared Josh is going to beat you," Sam added.

"Scared?" Amos asked with a growl. He lunged forward, making Sam leap back in fright. The bigger boy grinned. "I ain't scared of nothin', especially no uncontrollable triceratops."

"I can control him just fine!" Josh said.

"No, you can't," Amos said. He grinned, showing his crusty yellow teeth. "No one can. That's why O'Donnell wanted rid of him so bad."

Josh's jaw dropped. "How do you know about that?"

"Because I tipped him off, that's how!" Amos

laughed. "Everyone knows O'Donnell's a fraud-ster, and I knew just where he could find himself a gullible fool who'd be happy to take a crazy dinosaur off his hands."

Beside him, Arthur frowned. "Why did he have a dinosaur on his hands? That must've hurt."

"Shut up, Arthur!" Amos snapped.

"Shutting up now," said Arthur, bowing three or four times quickly.

Amos clapped his hands, and Clubber stomped toward them. "Face it. You got yourself a dud." He laughed, climbing onto the ankylosaurus's back. "See you on race day, losers."

"*Losers!*" Arthur giggled, scurrying after Clubber as he turned and lumbered away from the school. "Hilarious!"

Josh watched them go, then turned and looked Charge up and down. He'd been tricked. The triceratops was untamable.

He turned to Sam and Abi, who had worry written all over their faces.

"What am I gonna do now?"

CHAPTER 7

Josh sat up in bed and rubbed his eyes. He'd just been dreaming about riding through the Roaring Jaws Valley when he was woken by a loud screeching noise outside.

"What the…?"

It was pitch-dark—the middle of the night—but he was sure he'd heard…

Kaaaark!

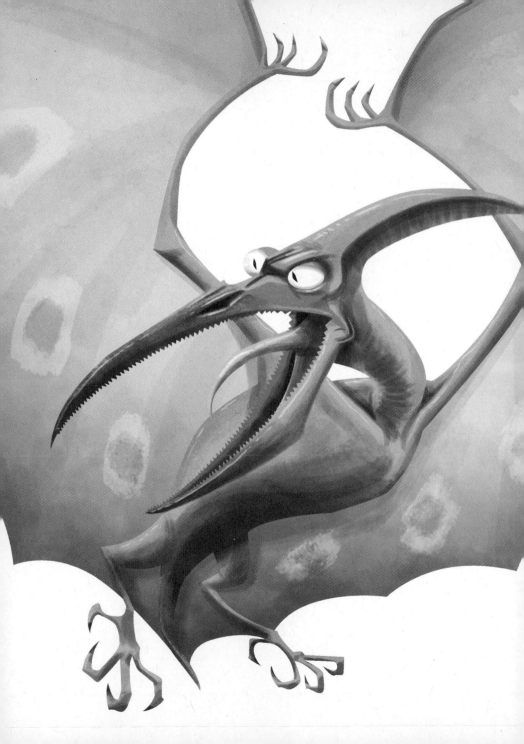

"Pterodactyl!" Josh cried. He'd know that sound anywhere.

He raced to the window and looked out just in time to see one of the winged beasts swoop down low over the barn, where some newly born iguanodons were being kept. It clattered against the roof, tearing at the wood with its claws.

If that thing got in the barn, those baby guanos were done for.

He leaped out of bed and jumped straight out of his window, racing for Plodder's pen. Nothing and no one was going to snatch up one of his family's iguanodons. There was no time to lose. The old gallimimus roared with surprise as Josh jumped on his back, then they raced out into the open, across to the barn.

"Get away from there!" Josh cried, waving his arms above his head and readying his lasso. The pterodactyl swooped down low and stretched its claws in his direction. In an instant, Plodder reared up in fright, throwing Josh off his back.

Josh hit the ground hard, knocking the wind from him. He could just make out the terrified cries of Plodder as he ran back to his pen.

"Plod!" he said and groaned. "Come back!" But it was no use. As he looked up into the sky, his eyes went wide with fear. The pterodactyl was plunging from the sky toward him. Its claws sliced through the air like knife blades.

And Josh had nowhere to run. He braced himself for impact...

Suddenly, a roar went up from his side, and a huge shadow passed over him. Three pointed horns stabbed upward at the pterodactyl.

"Charge!" Josh gasped.

The huge triceratops roared angrily as he swiped and slashed at the sky, forcing the winged dinosaur to flap higher into the air.

Josh jumped up, keeping a close eye on the 'dactyl. He felt something brush against his legs and looked down to see a large horn rising up from the ground toward him. Josh yelped in fright as he tumbled backward and then landed heavily on a pair of muscular shoulders.

Beneath him, Charge snorted, as if telling Josh to hold on. Josh grabbed the young dino's horns just as it kicked into top gear. The ground rolled by in a blur as Charge raced after the fleeing pterodactyl—with Plodder charging back in the other direction toward the ranch.

"I guess you don't like 'dactyls much," Josh said and laughed, barely able to believe it. He'd hoped if he'd found something Charge liked, the triceratops would let Josh ride him. He hadn't thought about trying to find something he *didn't* like!

Up in the air, the 'dactyl took one look at

the charging triceratops and flapped faster. To Josh's amazement, Charge lowered his head and quickly began to close the gap.

"Faster than a bullet in a hurricane!" Josh cheered.

Panicked, the 'dactyl turned and tried to swipe at them with its claws, but Charge reared up onto his hind legs, stabbing at the sky with his horns.

Josh whooped excitedly and held on tight. The pterodactyl gave an angry squawk, then flew straight up into the clouds.

"You did it!" Josh called. But as the flying dino took to the skies, Charge didn't stop charging. Now that he was all excited, he was zooming around like a dinosaur possessed—just as Mr. Sanders came running down from the house.

"Uh-oh," Josh said, but it was no use. Charge was heading right for the barn.

Luckily, Josh knew exactly what to do.

In an instant, he jumped up to standing on Charge's back, just like he'd done with Plodder. This time though, he took his lasso and looped it around Charge's huge central horn. With a yank of the rope, he shifted the dinosaur's head to the left. Just as he was about to crash into the side of the barn, the charging dino gave a roar and came to a shuddering stop. His dad looked on wide-eyed, face-to-face with the heaving, eager dino.

"Dad! Charge saved the guanos!" Josh cheered.

"And, look, I got him under control too." Charge gave an impatient snort. "Well, kinda!"

Mr. Sanders watched Josh, openmouthed. Eventually though, he gave him a wry smile. "Well, son, in all the years of dino wrangling, I've never seen anyone ride a trihorn like that. I guess you got yourself the new dino you were after," he said.

"Does that mean I get to race him?" Josh asked.

"I suppose it does," his dad began. "But on one condition—"

"Anything!" Josh said.

His dad cast an eye over what Josh was wearing. "No racing in your pajamas!"

The next morning, Josh couldn't wait to get going. The events of the night before were still fresh in his mind. He hadn't bought a dud dino after all—Amos had been wrong. Charge was crazy and willful, but he was as loyal as they came. And now he'd proved he could look after the guanos, his mom and dad had let him enter the race. As soon as he'd wolfed down breakfast though, he went to check on Plodder in the roundup barn.

"You're a mighty fine dinosaur, Plod," he said, giving the old gallimimus a pat on the neck. "But let's be honest, you ain't really built for racing. Sorry I kept trying to make you get faster. From now on, buddy, you just go at whatever speed you feel is best."

With a noisy *slurp*, Plodder licked Josh's face. "Ew. Thanks for that, pal," Josh said with a laugh. His old dinosaur seemed happy at the idea of going at his own speed for once.

Now, Josh could focus on getting Charge ready for the race. Even though he had Charge under control, the triceratops could go crazy at any minute. Just like when Josh daydreamed in class, Charge could be easily distracted. Josh needed something to keep the dino focused and ready for action. And he had just the right idea.

CHAPTER 8

L adies and gentlemen," cried the deputy mayor, silencing the gathered crowd. "Welcome to the hundredth anniversary of the Trihorn settlement and the great Founders' Day race!"

The audience broke into whoops and cheers as Mr. Geary introduced the festivities. The whole of Trihorn had been decked out with banners and ribbons, and it seemed like everyone from the Wandering Mountains to the Loneheart Lakes had turned out for the day of fun. The race was due to begin outside the town hall, go out into the Lost Plains, and finish back in Trihorn right where it began.

Over near the starting line, Josh was pacing anxiously. Since he'd found himself a faster dinosaur, Mr. Geary had let him race, but he was still nervous. His dad's words of wisdom rung in his ears, and his mom's breakfast pie churned in his belly.

"Don't get trampled into little bits," his dad had said.

"I don't want my good pie going to waste!" his mom added.

He'd promised them he'd be fine, but as he

looked at the other racers, he suddenly wasn't so sure. They were a fearsome-looking bunch, and they were riding some pretty fast dinosaurs. One of them was even sitting on the back of a velociraptor. It had a muzzle to keep its snapping jaws in place, but it still looked hungrily around at the crowd.

"Why can't they just start the race already?" Josh muttered.

"Calm down," Abi urged. "No point freaking out about it."

Josh knew his friend was right, but he could feel his nerves building. What if Charge went crazy? What if he couldn't keep him under control? But then a day ago, he hadn't even expected to be in the race. At least he was here.

"Still no sign of Terrordactyl Bill," said Sam, standing on a fruit box to let him see over the heads of the crowd.

But suddenly, there was no time for Josh to worry about where his hero was. The deputy mayor finally finished talking and ordered the racers to approach the line.

"Good luck!" called Sam and Abi as Josh swung into Charge's saddle.

"Yeah. You'll need it," a voice said. Josh turned to see Amos and his brute of an ankylosaur pull up to the starting line.

"Eat my dust, Amos," said Josh.

Amos glared darkly. "Watch what you're saying, or you'll eat my fist!"

Josh remembered his plan. Reaching into

his saddlebag, he took out a contraption made of string and leather. Charge grunted as Josh fastened it around the dinosaur's enormous head.

"Relax, buddy," Josh said. "They're just blinders to stop you getting distracted and charging off anywhere." He positioned two of the leather flaps near Charge's eyes, blocking his view of everything going on beside him. Charge loved to run fast, but it was time he did it when *Josh* wanted him to.

Josh took the reins again just as the starting gun was fired and the ribbon dropped. A dozen dinosaurs thundered forward, leaving the cheering crowd behind.

"Go, Charge, go!" Josh cried, digging his knees into his dino's sides. The triceratops bounded across the dusty ground, picking up speed with every step.

As they raced toward the creek, the other riders were pulling ahead. Josh glanced back over his shoulder, fearing he was in last place, and was pleased to see Amos and Clubber rumbling along a short distance behind.

"See you at the finish line, Amos!" Josh called, then he ducked low and gave Charge an encouraging, "Yah!"

A herd of grazing iguanodons was gathered in the creek, munching on its grassy banks. They looked up in surprise as twelve fast-moving dinosaurs hurtled toward them, led by a snarling velociraptor. The first few riders dodged through the herd without any problem, but by the time Josh reached them, the iguanodons were stampeding in panic.

"You can do it, buddy," Josh said, but Charge didn't need the encouragement. He pushed on, dodging and weaving through the stampeding herd. Josh cracked his lasso like a whip, and they cut right through the stampede.

With a triumphant roar, Charge made it through the herd. Josh guided him to the right, following the race route. The course arced in a wide circle, right around the town and out onto the Lost Plains. Soon though, they were headed toward the old dinosaur graveyard.

Josh and Charge dashed into the dusty canyon and were immediately dwarfed by the towering piles of dinosaur bones on all sides. Bleached rib cages and leering skulls loomed over them as Josh and Charge ran in the direction of the T. rex skeleton at the graveyard's center.

The T. rex's bones were enormous, towering over both Josh and Charge. The race route took them right through the skeleton's back legs. Even though it was long dead, Josh's heart still raced at the sheer size of it. Even Charge seemed to miss a beat when he spotted the skull's huge jaws, but he picked up speed again when Josh rubbed the top of his head.

"That's it, Charge. You can do it," Josh encouraged.

As they dived through the towering bones, Josh heard a mean cry and a loud grunt from behind. He looked over his shoulder and saw

Amos yanking his reins and deliberately sending Clubber's huge spiky tail smashing into Charge.

"Watch it!" Josh shouted, glaring at Amos.

Amos grinned and pointed up. "No, *you'd* better watch it. Yah!"

Charge staggered sideways. Caught off balance, he smashed into one of the T. rex's

rib bones. As Clubber and Amos dashed ahead, Josh looked up and gasped. The T. rex's huge rib cage swung down, the sharp bones stabbing toward them.

Josh could only close his eyes and hold on tight. There was a crash from all sides, and Charge came shuddering to a halt. When Josh opened his eyes, he saw Amos laughing as he raced away on Clubber and the T. rex's fallen rib cage surrounding him and Charge like an enormous cage.

"Oh no!" Josh cried. "We're trapped!"

CHAPTER 9

Amos and the other riders were now just a cloud of dust at the far end of the dino graveyard. Josh reached over and shook one of the bone bars of their prison, but it wouldn't budge. T. rex bones were as solid as they looked.

"We're stuck," Josh cried. After all he'd done to get this far, it was a dead dinosaur that had stopped him in his tracks!

But Charge wasn't having any of it. He lifted his head into the air and snorted. The dinosaur took three steps backward so his huge backside was pressed against one side of the rib cage.

Josh realized what the triceratops was planning just in the nick of time. Charge was going to smash his way out of there. Josh ducked low,

taking cover behind the dino's tough fringe as Charge charged. His armored skull smashed into the bones like a battering ram, splintering them into a thousand pieces.

"Nice one, Charge," Josh called. "We're back in the race!"

Charge's feet chewed up the ground as Josh guided him along the track. In no time, Charge had caught up with Amos and Clubber.

"Takes more than a dead T. rex to stop us," Josh yelled with a laugh as he and Charge left the bully behind.

"Come back here, you..." Amos started, but his voice soon trailed off into the distance.

The next obstacle was over by the town's rodeo pen. Charge skidded around a rocky bend and caught up with the other dinosaurs leaping over rows of barrels.

"Oh great. Jumps." Josh groaned. He had visions of Charge stomping through the barrels, crushing them with his huge feet.

Josh didn't need to worry. As they hurtled toward the first barrel, he pulled on the reins, and Charge gracefully threw himself into the air like a scaly ballerina. For a moment, the world seemed to go very quiet. Josh felt like he was flying.

Then Charge's feet slammed against the hard ground, and they were running again. Another tug. Another leap. Another floating sensation. And then another *boom* as Charge hit the ground.

By the time Charge had cleared the last jump, he and Josh had made it into fourth place. There was only a sprint through the ravine outside of town to go until the finish line. Josh gritted his teeth and ducked low in the saddle. Charge let out a low grumble as they sped through the shadows of the ravine. Long, spindly black rocks hung over them like fingers getting ready to grab. Plumes of choking smoke rose up from tar pits on either side of the track, stinging Josh's eyes and sending toxic fumes spiraling up his nostrils. Every instinct told him he should turn back.

"Would T-Bill turn back?" he whispered to himself. "Not a chance."

Josh pressed on, sending Charge scrambling

up a steep hill. The dinosaur roared as he saw the velociraptor speeding ahead of him. The triceratops bounded along the narrow track, and Josh had to pull on the reins to keep him steady. They were going fast but still nowhere near as fast as they'd gone out in the open. Running at top speed was too risky. One false move, and Charge would fall down the slope.

But then the track leveled off, and Josh could see the canyon exit looming ahead. With a kick of Josh's boot, Charge put on a burst of speed and zoomed past the fierce rider.

"Let's show Amos what we've got," Josh said, clapping Charge on the shoulder. The dinosaur snorted, lowered his head, and ran.

Josh ducked low as the wind whipped at

him. The canyon walls were passing in a blur of speed. Charge's feet were chewing up the ground, getting faster and faster with every frantic bound.

With a triumphant roar, Charge exploded from the canyon and skidded around the bend. It was a straight run to the finish line, and there were only two riders up ahead.

"Woo-hoo!" Josh yelped as Charge kicked off with his powerful back legs. The whistling air stung at his eyes and blew his hat clean off his head as Charge thundered on. He was faster than any triceratops Josh had ever seen. Faster, perhaps, than any dinosaur ever!

Feeling the ground shake beneath him, Charge closed in on the other riders. Suddenly, the sky darkened, and a familiar shape passed over the sun.

"Pterodactyl!" Josh gasped, grabbing tight on the reins. But he didn't have to worry— Charge completely ignored the winged dino. Josh's homemade blinders were working!

They weaved left as they passed another rider, with only one racer up ahead. The finish line was nearing, and Josh could hear the cheering of the crowds as he and Charge made their way through the Trihorn settlement.

There was only one rider left to beat, but they were closing on the finish line fast. Josh held his breath.

With a roar, Charge kicked out, launching him toward the finish line, neck and neck with a gallimimus. Both dinosaurs landed on the ground together, and Josh spun in the saddle, waiting for the verdict.

"In first place…by a horn," began the deputy mayor, and Josh broke into a grin. "Josh Sanders on Charge!"

Sliding out of the saddle, Josh threw his arms in the air. "We did it, Charge!"

Sam and Abi came over to congratulate him as Amos finally trundled over the line. He had a face like a meteorite was about to strike the Earth.

Josh turned to see a tall, muscular man staring down at him. His jaw dropped as the man held out a powerful hand for him to shake.

"Name's Terrordactyl Bill," the man said.

Josh's mouth flapped open and closed. "I...I know," he said.

"That there was some mighty fine racing," said T-Bill. "Reckon I couldn't have done much better myself."

"You could!" Josh said quickly. "You totally could! You're the greatest dino rider ever!"

T-Bill smiled. "For now, maybe. But you're going to be chasing that crown before I know it." He tapped Josh on the head. "Speaking of crowns, looks like you lost yours."

Josh felt for his hat and realized it wasn't there. "It must've blown off," he said, panicked. "It was a replica of yours."

"Well, why have a replica?" T-Bill asked. "I think you've earned the real thing."

Josh gawped as T-Bill took off his hat and placed it on Josh's head. Suddenly, the crowd was swarming around them, and Josh was hoisted up onto his dad's shoulders.

"My son, the dino rider," his dad cheered, and the crowd cheered with him. Sam and Abi looked on and cheered too.

Josh looked down at the smiling faces of the

townsfolk and at Charge, who chomped happily on a patch of grass. This was the greatest day of his life, but he had a feeling his adventures with Charge had only just begun!

Don't miss Josh's next adventure in

How to Rope a Giganotosaurus

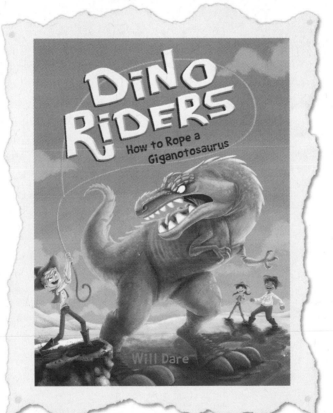

CHAPTER

1

It was early evening, and the sun was beginning its slow creep down the sky. Josh Sanders and his friends, Sam and Abi, were moseying on into town. They had money in their pockets, errands to run, and several tons of dinosaur plodding along beneath them. It was just another day in Trihorn County, and Josh was hungry for adventure.

"Race you into town," he suggested. Charge,

his triceratops, gave an excited snort. It had only been a few weeks since Josh had ridden the 'cera in the Founders' Day race, and they'd both been itching for another dose of excitement ever since.

Abi and Sam looked down at their own dinosaurs. They each rode their own gallimimus—a long-necked dinosaur, which was capable of some impressive bursts of speed.

"Deal," said Abi.

"See you at the finish line," Sam laughed, then he and Abi kicked their heels, spurring their dinosaurs into action.

"Hey, wait, no fair!" Josh cried as his friends sped off toward Trihorn settlement. He leaned forward in the saddle and whispered into Charge's ear, "You ready, buddy?"

Charge snorted and nodded his enormous head. Josh patted him on one of his horns and then straightened up. "Let's at least give them a head start," he said, a sly grin creeping across his face. "Three…two…one…go!"

Josh gripped the reins as Charge shot forward, the dino's powerful feet thundering across the dry ground. Josh thought back to the frantic sprint to the finish line he and Charge had made in the Founders' Day race. He'd only owned Charge for a few days before the race, but that hadn't stopped Josh from riding to victory.

The world whistled by in a blur of brown and blue. Sam and Abi both turned in their saddles as Charge powered up behind them. They stood in their stirrups, flicking the reins as fast as they could, but no matter how fast their dinosaurs ran, they were no match for the triceratops.

"Last one to the store's a diplodocus dropping!" Josh grinned wildly, thundering past.

Charge raced along Main Street, dodging past a group of dinos tied to a tethering post outside the saloon, then slowing for a moment

as they passed the sheriff's office. The sheriff didn't much approve of dinosaurs running down Main Street. Then again, he didn't much approve of anything.

Charge gave a final burst of speed, then skidded to a halt outside the town store. He stopped so abruptly, his back legs lifted off the ground, and Josh had to grab on to the dino's armored

fringe to stop himself from being flung through the air.

Josh swung out of the saddle just as Sam and Abi trotted up. They and their dinosaurs were all breathing heavily, while Charge had barely broken a sweat.

"Argh, I miscalculated the turn trajectories!" Sam protested. "I'd have won if I hadn't done that."

Charge turned and loudly bottom-burped in Sam's direction. Josh pinched his nose and laughed. "I think Charge disagrees!"

Sam wrinkled his nose and jumped out of the way of the toxic gas.

"All righty then," said Abi. "What are we here for again?"

"My dad's errands," Josh said with a groan as he began to make his way toward the general store. "C'mon, let's get it over with…"

Suddenly though, he stopped as he spotted a large crowd gathered along the street. Molly, a girl from school, stood in the middle of the group, passing out copies of the *Daily Diplodocus* newspaper that were being eagerly snatched out of her hands.

"What's all the hubbub?" Abi asked, swinging down from her dino.

Josh shrugged. "Only one way to find out, I guess."

ABOUT THE AUTHOR

Ever since he was a little boy, Will Dare has been mad about T. rexes and velociraptors. He always wondered what it would be like to live in a world where they were still alive. Now, grown up, he has put pen to paper and imagined just that world. Will lives in rural America with his wife and best pal, Charge (a dog, not a triceratops).